Something's Hiding

Written by Judy Nayer
Illustrated by Steve Henry

WILLOWISP PRESS

Published by Willowisp Press
801 94th Avenue North, St. Petersburg, Florida 33702

Printed in the United States of America.
A Creative Media Applications Production.

ISBN 0-87406-792-8

10 9 8 7 6 5 4 3 2 1

Something's hiding
under my rug.
It's tiny and round.
I think it's a. . .

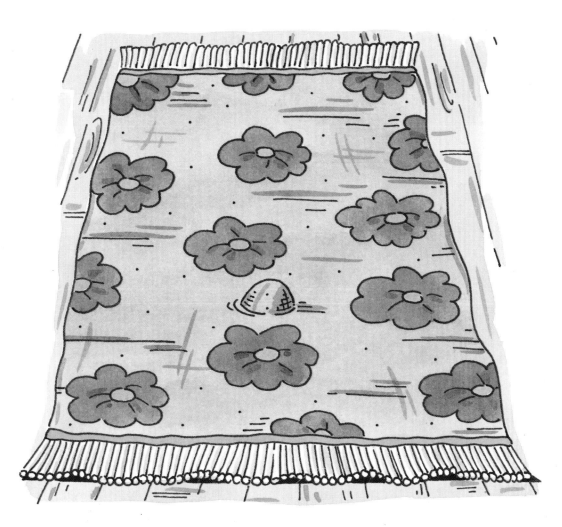

Something's hiding
in my house.
It's little and gray.
I think it's a. . .

Something's hiding
in my hat.
It's orange and fluffy.
I think it's a. . .

Something's hiding
in my log.
It's spotted and brown.
I think it's a. . .

Something's hiding
in my box.
It's furry and red.
I think it's a. . .

Something's hiding
in my jeep.
It's woolly and white.
I think it's a. . .

Something's hiding
behind my door.
It's huge and green.
It's a. . .

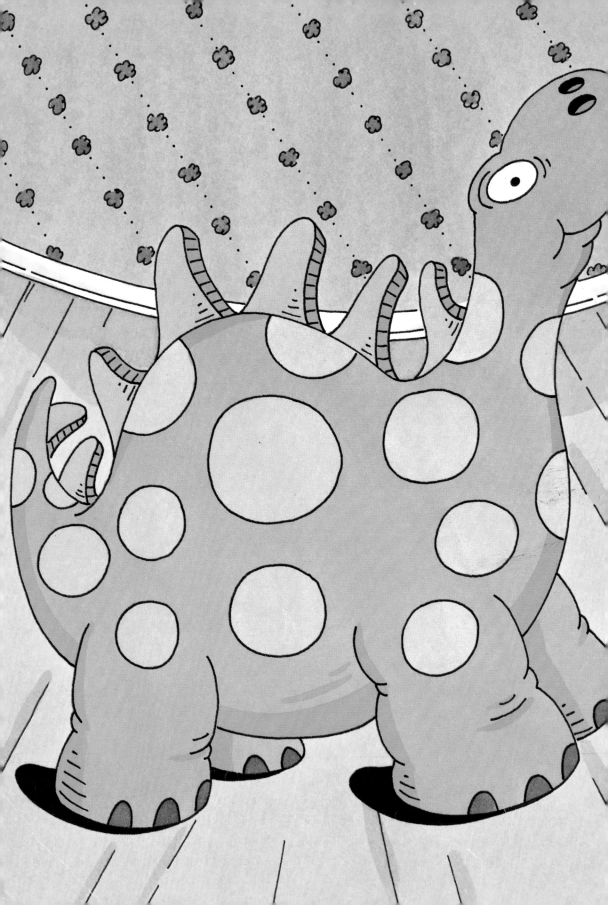